Copyright © 2001 by Michael Neugebauer Verlag, an imprint of Nord-Süd Verlag AG, Gossau Zürich, Switzerland.
First published in Switzerland under the title *Mama, ich hab dich lieb*.
English translation copyright © 2001 by North-South Books Inc.
All rights reserved. No part of this book may be reproduced or utilized in any form or by any means, electronic
or mechanical, including photocopying, recording, or any information storage and retrieval system, without
permission in writing from the publisher.
First published in the United States, Great Britain, Canada, Australia, and New Zealand in 2001 by North-South
Books, an imprint of Nord-Süd Verlag AG, Gossau Zürich, Switzerland. First paperback edition published in
2005 by North-South Books. Distributed in the United States by North-South Books Inc., New York.

Library of Congress Cataloging-in-Publication Data
Loupy, Christophe.
Hugs and Kisses / Christophe Loupy, Eve Tharlet; translated by J. Alison James.
p. cm.
"A Michael Neugebauer book."
Summary: Hugs the puppy sets out to collect lots of wonderful kisses from his animal friends,
but in the end he discovers that the best kiss of all is the one he gets from his loving mother.
[1. Kissing—Fiction. 2. Dogs—Fiction. 3. Animals—Fiction. 4. Mother and child—Fiction.]
I. Tharlet, Eve. II. James, J. Alison. III. Title.
PZ7.L95435 Mam 2002 [E]—dc21 2001042595
A CIP catalogue record for this book is available from The British Library.
ISBN 0-7358-1484-8 (trade edition) 10 9 8 7 6 5
ISBN 0-7358-1485-6 (library edition) 10 9 8 7 6 5 4 3 2 1
ISBN 0-7358-1972-6 (paperback edition) 10 9 8 7 6 5 4 3 2 1
Printed in Belgium

For more information about our books, and the authors and artists
who create them, visit our web site: www.northsouth.com

Christophe Loupy **Hugs**
and Kisses

Eve Tharlet

Translated by J. Alison James

A MICHAEL NEUGEBAUER BOOK
NORTH-SOUTH BOOKS / NEW YORK / LONDON

One morning, Hugs the puppy woke up early. His mother and father and all his sisters were still sleeping. Quietly he tiptoed outside. There was something he had to find out.

"Good morning," called two ducks from the pond.
"What are you doing up so early?"
"I'm finding out something," Hugs said. "Could you
  please give me a kiss?"
"A kiss?" quacked the ducks. "Of course. Where would
  you like it?"
"Right here," said Hugs, and he pointed to his cheek.

So the ducks came out of the water and each gave him a kiss: one on the left and one on the right.
Hugs closed his eyes and smiled. He'd never ever had a kiss from a duck!
It was a bit hard of course, and wet, but it was quite refreshing.
Hugs thanked the ducks and went on.

Out in the pasture Hugs saw a horse. "Good morning!" he called.

"Good morning," answered the horse. "It's nice of you to visit."

"I was wondering," Hugs said shyly. "Could you please give me a kiss?"

"A kiss?" neighed the horse.

"Yes, right here." Hugs pointed to his forehead.

So the horse bent down
and gave him a big kiss.
Hugs closed his eyes and
smiled. He'd never ever had
a kiss from a horse!
It was a bit damp of course,
and sticky, but it was
quite warm.
Hugs thanked the horse
and went on.

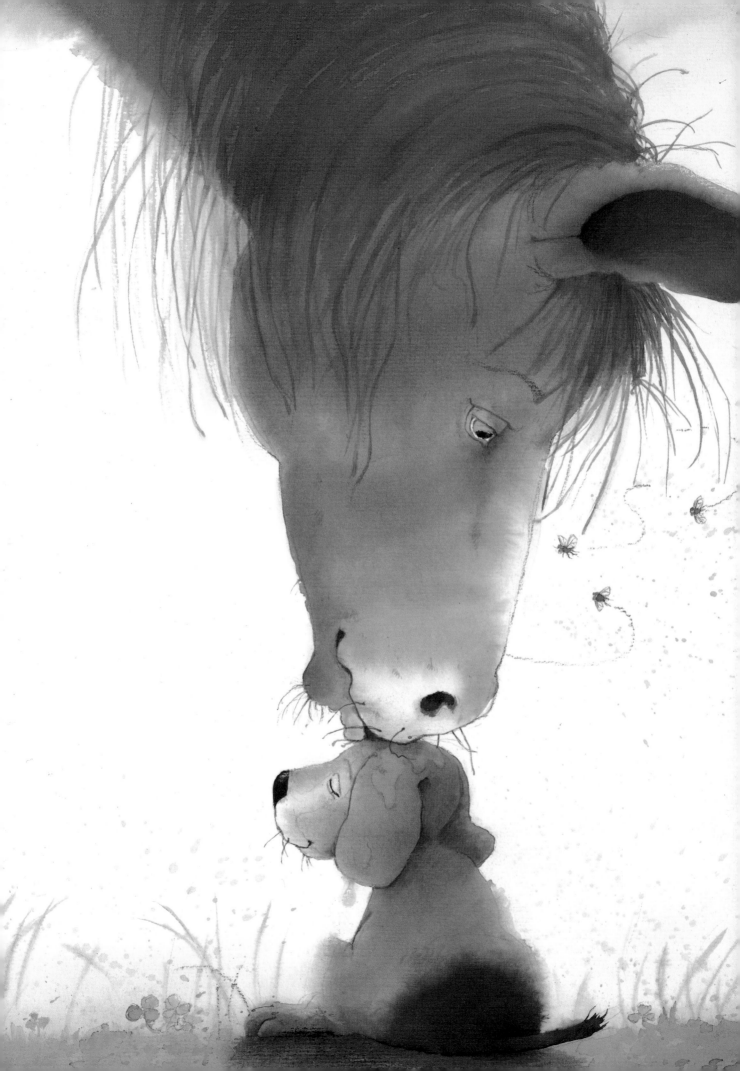

Soon the puppy found a pig rolling in a puddle of mud.

"Good morning," said Hugs.

"Good morning to you," answered the pig. "What are you doing here all alone?"

"I'm finding out something," Hugs said. "Could you please give me a kiss?"

"A kiss from me?" grunted the pig.

"Yes, right here." Hugs pointed to the tip of his nose.

So the pig stepped out of the mud and gave him a kiss
right on the tip of his nose.
Hugs closed his eyes and smiled. He'd never ever had a
kiss from a pig!
It was a bit muddy of course, and the bristles scratched
a little, but it was quite tender.
Hugs thanked the pig and went on.

Hugs came to a garden fence. There he spied a rabbit out among the corn.

"Good morning," he called.

"What are you doing so far from home?" asked the rabbit.

"I'm finding out something," Hugs said. "Could you please give me a kiss?"

"A kiss from me?" murmured the rabbit.

"Yes, right here." Hugs pointed to his neck.

The rabbit hopped closer and gave him a kiss right in his wrinkled fur.

Hugs closed his eyes and smiled. He'd never ever had a kiss from a rabbit!

It was a bit wiggley of course, and quick, but it was quite soft.

Hugs thanked the rabbit and headed back home.

On the way, Hugs saw a yellow butterfly.

"Good morning," he called.

"Morning, morning!" whispered the butterfly in the wind.

"You have been out for a long time!"

"I'm heading home," Hugs said. "But first, could you give me a kiss?"

"A kiss from me?" The butterfly dipped his wings.

"Yes, please, a kiss right here." Hugs pointed to his mouth.

So the butterfly settled gently on
his mouth and gave him a kiss.
Hugs closed his eyes again and
smiled. Oh, so fine, a butterfly's kiss!
He'd never felt anything like it before.
It tickled a bit of course, but it
was wonderful.
Hugs thanked the butterfly with
all his heart and hurried on home.

His mother and father and sisters were all waiting for him.

"Where have you been?" asked Mother. "We were worried about you."

"Oh, it was such a beautiful morning, I couldn't sleep. And there was something I had to find out."

"Now my little one, what was so important?" Mother nuzzled Hugs and gave him a big kiss.

"That's it!" Hugs said. "Now I know:
A kiss from a duck is refreshing.
A kiss from a horse is warm,
A kiss from a pig is tender,
A kiss from a rabbit is soft,
A kiss from a butterfly is wonderful…
But the best kiss of all is the kiss I get from you!"